2521

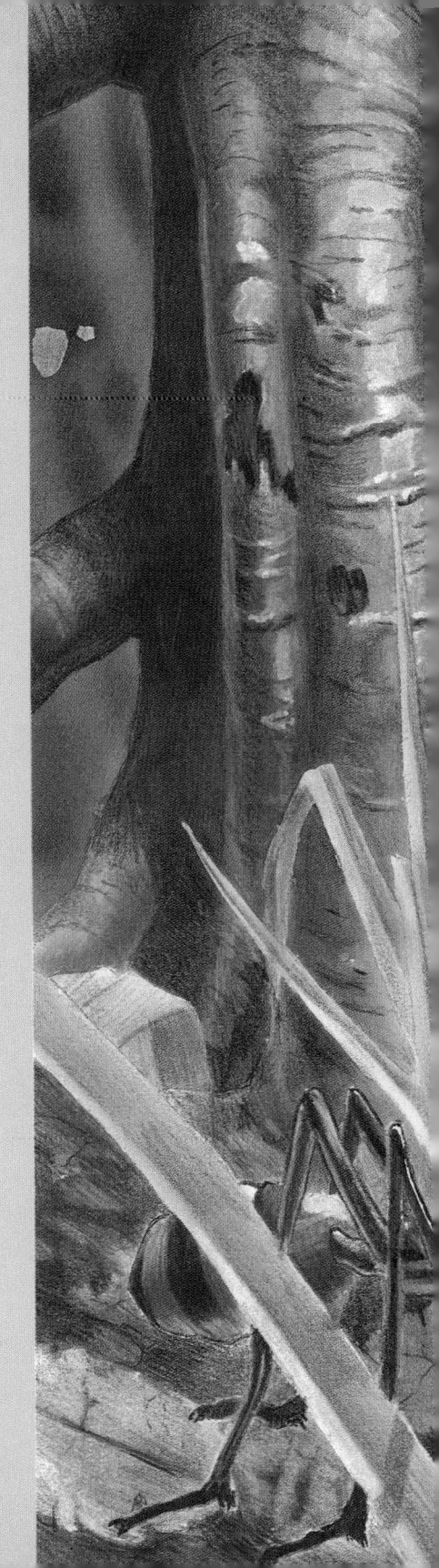

KRYPTIC

THE LITTLE SPACE GUY

Story and illustration by
Gregg Rodgers

Written by
Norman Shrive

Designed by
Dave Lukas

Cyril Hayes Press Inc.
3312 Mainway, Burlington, Ontario L7M 1A7
One Colomba Drive, Niagara Falls, New York 14305

Far, far off, in the immense, mysterious blackness of space, a pinpoint of brightness was moving at tremendous speed. It was not a falling star, for falling stars disappear very quickly, but something very, very small, almost tiny, flashing across the cloudless sky. Past millions of faraway stars, suns and planets it flew, its shiny shape gliding by the moon, sometimes missing the moon mountains only by inches.

What was it? Where had it come from? Where was it going?

Inside the spaceship a spaceman was anxiously peering from first one porthole and then another. His name was Kryptic (which is space language for "little space guy"), and he was not quite sure where he was.

Not lost, mind you, but a little confused.

Suddenly, there was a planet below him that in the light of the sun and the moon was like a beautiful blue, green and silver ball. Kryptic took out his space map and looked at it carefully. Then he looked at it again. And again. At last he said, "This planet must be Earth. I shall land and be the first of my kind to explore this pretty blue marble."

So down came the spaceship, down, down, down, until it landed — thud! — in a lovely forest, all green with trees and plants, and red, yellow, purple with pretty leaves and flowers.

Kryptic nervously opened his sliding door, looked carefully both left and right, then, one by one, placed his bi-pods (which is space language for "round metal feet") on the soft, mossy earth.

Oh, he said to himself, how different is this world from mine! Above his head was the four-petaled face of a pretty purple flower. Nearby, around huge towering trees, were great brown and black mushrooms, their wide heads spreading like thick umbrellas. There came the strange sounds of chitters, chirps and cheeps.

"Wow!" said Kryptic, "neat, really neat."

He carefully lifted his left bi-pod and took a step. Then another. In no time he was quite sure of himself.

Suddenly, one of his bi-pods slipped on the damp moss, and down, down he fell, rolling over and over until - thump! he was stopped by a great soft lump! The great soft lump gave out a snort! Kryptic turned cold with terror! What was it? Oh, dear, he had never before seen anything like it! It was so grim and gray, so large and leathery, so absolutely ugh! and ugly.

"What are you?" grumbled the great gray toad. Of all the insects I have seen in my woods, I have never seen one like you." And he gave another terrible snort.

He was indeed a cruel toad. As poor Krytpic stood there, so frightened that his IC (his Internal Calculator) clicked and clattered, Toad growled, "Well, it doesn't matter. I have just had a nice lunch of insects; you will be a special dessert!"

"I'm sssorry!" squeaked Kryptic, shaking like a leaf, "bbut I'm not an insect, wwhatever that is; I'm a space visitor - from up there!" And he pointed a shaking, shiny finger to the sky.

"It makes no difference to me," grunted Toad. "Many of my favorite insect dishes come from up there, as you call it, so why should you be so special?"

Then suddenly, because by now Kryptic was paralyzed with fright and no longer shaking, Toad could not see him! So, as Toad turned his head and rolled his egg-like eyes, hoping to find Kryptic, the little space guy pressed both bi-pods into the turf and leaped right over Toad!

Oh, how Kryptic's little legs moved! Sometimes trying to run through the leaves, logs and lumps of rock, other times using his BURPS (his Bi-pod Upward and Reverse Propulsion System), he bounded over the brush and boggy ground. Behind him he could hear Toad crashing after him.

hen, as if from nowhere, there appeared a gently flowing, happily gurgling stream. As quick as a flash Kryptic picked up a piece of bark, pushed it into the water, and jumping neatly onto the bark, sailed away from the bank. As he rounded a bend in the stream, he looked back and saw Toad, glaring and gasping, on the very spot he had just left.

"I've fooled him this time," he said to himself, feeling much safer by now. "But I still have to get back to my spaceship and he will be watching for me."

As he floated down the silvery stream, Kryptic had time once again to look at the beautiful world he had come to.

He was wakened from his day-dreaming by the water becoming rough and choppy. Then it began to crash and boil in great waves and whirlpools. As the raft plunged and reared, Kryptic noticed that the water ahead seemed to disappear: everything beyond was trees and sky. Suddenly the raft hit a wave and it tilted up so high that Kryptic was thrown into the air, turning a complete somersault before landing on his bi-pods right on the edge of a waterfall!

O h, dear," sighed Kryptic, "it was never like this back home, where every morning a program card was inserted into my IC and everything was worked out carefully beforehand."   Kryptic was tired from his long journey and all his adventures afterward. His EEK (his Energy Element Kapsule - note that spacemen and scientists spell "capsule" with a "K") had begun to run down, and needed a little peace and quiet in order to re-charge itself.

"I think I'll have a rest," said Kryptic, and he lay down on the soft moss. In nine seconds he was fast asleep, his IC beginning to click happily again.

Kryptic might have slept many hours if his BEEP (his Basic External Emergency Pager) had not sent a warning that something was touching him. He looked up cautiously, and there, staring at him, were two large eyes that were divided into many parts and surrounded by fur.

"Oh, dear, who are you?" he asked.

"My name is Ant," said the other. "Why have I not seen an insect like you before?"

"Because," replied Kryptic, "I am not an insect. I am a visitor from another planet. My name is Kryptic, which in my language means 'little space guy,' and I came in a spaceship."

"Very interesting," said Ant. But then he added, "I should like to see this marvelous machine. Take me to it and we can pick up some of my friends on the way. I'm sure they will be interested because, like me, they are very curious creatures." And, as if to prove his point, at that moment they were joined by Buzzz the Bee.

"Not so fast," Kryptic replied. "As spacemen often say, 'we have a problem!' There is a cruel toad who wants me for dessert and, quite frankly, that's as bad as being lost in outer space forever."

"More like being lost in inner space - Toad's inner space!" said Buzzz. "We know all about him, and for a long time we have tried to find a way to teach him a lesson. But he is so awesome and awful, so lumpy and loathsome, that we never succeed.

"I'll tell you what," said Kryptic. "I'll switch my IC to its 'Emergency Plan' position and, as we collect your friends, perhaps it will tell us how to handle Toad. Let's go!"

So that's what they did. Through the woods they went while Kryptic's IC clicked and Ant's many strange friends collected around them. And what curious creatures they were! And so many different kinds! Kryptic, even with his very clever brain, could not keep track of their names. Ants, both black and red; flies, both big and small; beetles, both brittle and soft. And all sorts of little flying fellows with wonderful glossy wings that hummed as they moved through the air just above Kryptic's head. Such colors they had! And such a symphony of sounds as they buzzed and bumbled, cheeped and chirped, all at the same time! Kryptic found it all quite brain-boggling, and hoped that it would not disturb the working of his IC!

At last they came to a small clearing about five meters from the spaceship. Kryptic could not actually see his craft, but his RIP (his Radar Indicator of Position) informed him it was there. His IC had given him a plan. With a quick touch of his BURPS, he leaped to the top of a mushroom and, facing his friends, he told them how they were going to deal with the abominable Toad.

"I believe," he said, "that in the past you have not been able to handle Toad because you have not worked together as a group. When you rush at him, even buzz or bash at him one by one, he is able to pick you off easily. I am sorry to hear that he has even had some of your friends and relatives for breakfast, lunch and dinner."

He then told them that they must work as a team, that while the ants were attacking Toad from the front, the beetles would come from behind. At the same time, the bees, wasps, hornets and ladybugs would come in like dive-bombers from above. That was the way they would defeat Toad!

At that moment, when everything seemed to be going well and everyone was happy with Kryptic's plan - crash! right into the middle of the clearing leaped the terrible Toad! Kryptic's friends scattered in all directions - tumbling, twisting, flying, fleeing, rolling, reeling, buzzing and humming in fear and fright! But it was Kryptic that Toad wanted first.

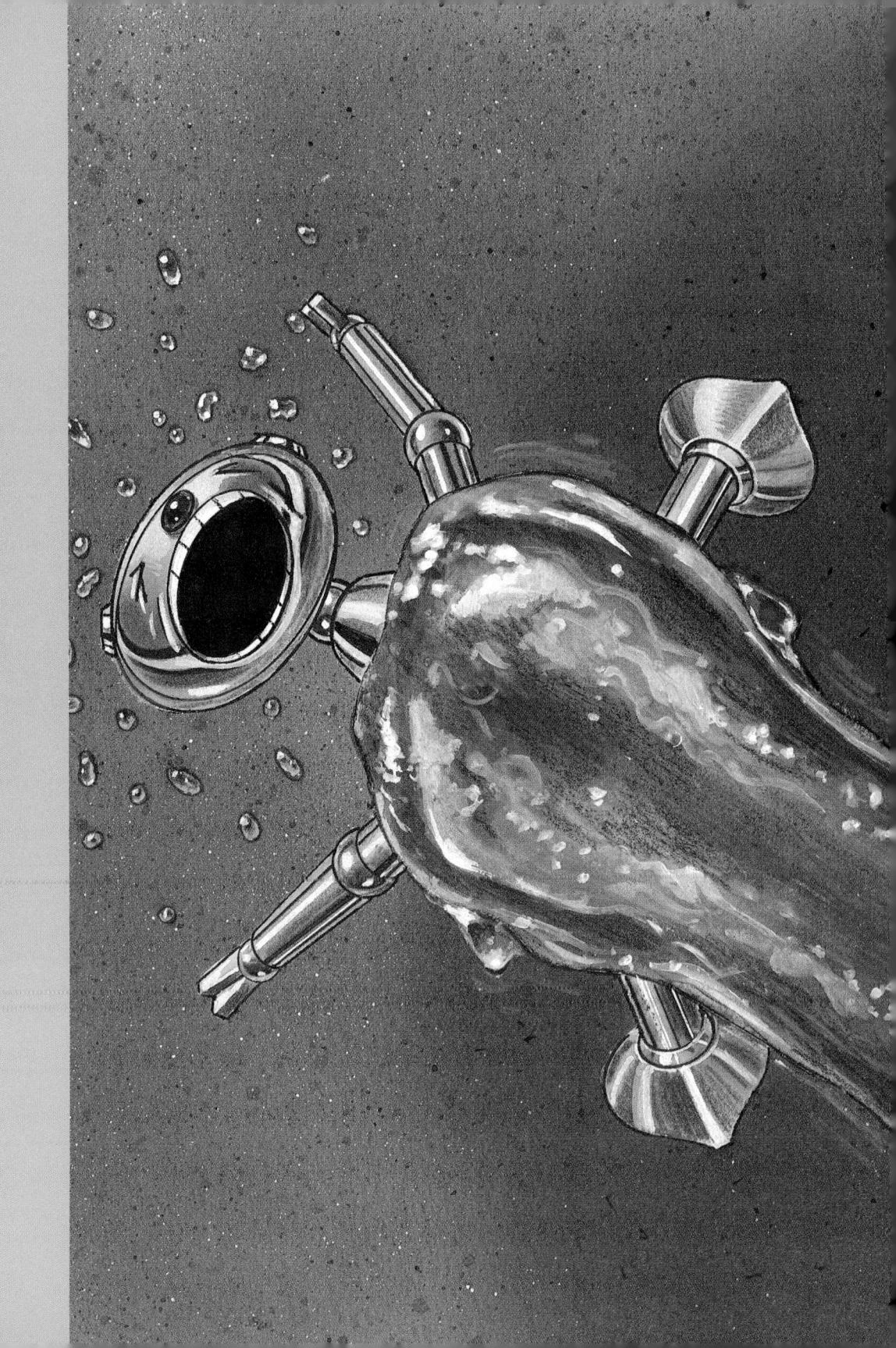

Kryptic had been knocked off his mushroom by a crashing daisy and, as he struggled to stand on his bi-pods, out flashed Toad's slithery, slimy tongue. In a twinkle Kryptic was in Toad's mouth! And only his bi-pods stopped him from sliding down into the terrible Toad's tummy! The insects stared in horror. Was their new friend gone forever? Were they now to suffer for daring to fight against Toad?

I

t was Ant who first came to his senses.

"Friends," he shouted, "remember what Kryptic told us! Form fast your formations and attack, attack!"

From all over the clearing the insects came. The ants assailed Toad from the front, the beetles bashed him at the back, and the bees, ladybugs and all those with wings zoomed down at him from above. And as Toad crouched and cringed, an amazing change came over him. His leathery skin began to sweat, his great glassy eyes began to bulge. Even steam began to seep out of his mouth!

"Aaaaargh!" he shrieked.

And as he did, out popped Kryptic!

"Quick!" said Kryptic, "roll him over and hold him down! Even stroke his tummy if that will help keep him quiet!"

And that's what they did. Toad lay flat on his back, his long, hind legs stretched out on the leaves and twigs. He was completely tired out. Never again would Toad believe that he owned the woods all to himself and that he could be cruel and mean whenever he felt like it.

The victory over Toad called for a big celebration. After lifting Kryptic onto their shoulders and giving three rousing cheers, his friends all began to dance and sing. Some of them jitterbugged, others did the buggy-wuggy. Caterpillars even did the twist. Overhead the bees buzzed as they never had before. And while they sang and danced, old Toad slunk off, thoroughly ashamed.

At last Kryptic said, "Dear friends, I must go. The sun is almost down, and I would like to get at least as far as the moon tonight. Come and see my spaceship, help me get aboard, and then wave me goodbye."

So they all went to where the spaceship waited. And because they were curious creatures, they had to spend some time inspecting the shiny little machine. Chirping, cheeping, buzzing and humming, they climbed under and over, in and out of, Kryptic's marvelous craft.

They formed a circle around it as he closed the door. They saw him activate his propulsion system and rise slowly and gently from their woods. The spaceship turned toward them as Kryptic waved goodbye once more. He pointed it upward toward the moon and accelerated rapidly away.

For a long time the insects watched as the spaceship became smaller and smaller. Then it became only a bright pinpoint among the stars, speeding toward the dark and mysterious sky!

The End.